If Wishes Were Horses

E. P. DUTTON • NEW YORK

MOTHER GOOSE
If Wishes Were Horses
AND OTHER RHYMES • ILLUSTRATED BY
SUSAN JEFFERS

Copyright © 1979 by Susan Jeffers

All rights reserved. No part of this publication may be reproduced or transmitted in any form or by any means, electronic or mechanical, including photocopy, recording, or any information storage and retrieval system now known or to be invented, without permission in writing from the publisher, except by a reviewer who wishes to quote brief passages in connection with a review written for inclusion in a magazine, newspaper, or broadcast.

Library of Congress Cataloging in Publication Data

Mother Goose. If wishes were horses.

SUMMARY: Presents rhymes about horses from Mother Goose.
1. Nursery rhymes. 2. Horses—Juvenile poetry.
[1. Nursery rhymes. 2. Horses—Poetry]
I. Jeffers, Susan. II. Title.
PZ8.3.M85Jc 1979 398.8 79-9986 ISBN 0-525-32531-X

Published in the United States by E. P. Dutton, a Division of Elsevier-Dutton Publishing Company, Inc., New York

Published simultaneously in Canada by Clarke, Irwin & Company Limited, Toronto and Vancouver

Editor: Ann Durell   Designer: Riki Levinson

Printed in the U.S.A.   First Edition
10 9 8 7 6 5 4 3 2 1

for Jane

for Auntie Sharon

If wishes were horses

Beggars would ride.

If daisies were watches
I'd wear one by my side.

Ride away!

Ride away!

Charlie shall ride.

He'll have a puppy tied to one side.

He'll have a kitten tied to the other,

and they will go riding

to see his grandmother.

This is the way the ladies ride—
Nimble, nimble, nimble.

This is the way the gentlemen ride—
Gallop and trot, gallop and trot.

And when they come upon a fence,
They jump UP over.

When they come upon a ditch,
They scramble DOWN below—

A farmer went trotting
Upon his good mare
Bumpety bumpety bump.

With his daughter behind him
So rosy and fair
Lumpety lumpety lump.

A raven cried Croak!
And they all tumbled down
Bumpety bumpety bump!

The mare skinned her knees
The farmer his crown
Lumpety lumpety lump!

The mischievous raven
Flew laughing away—

And vowed he would serve them
The same the next day...

Bumpety bumpety bump!

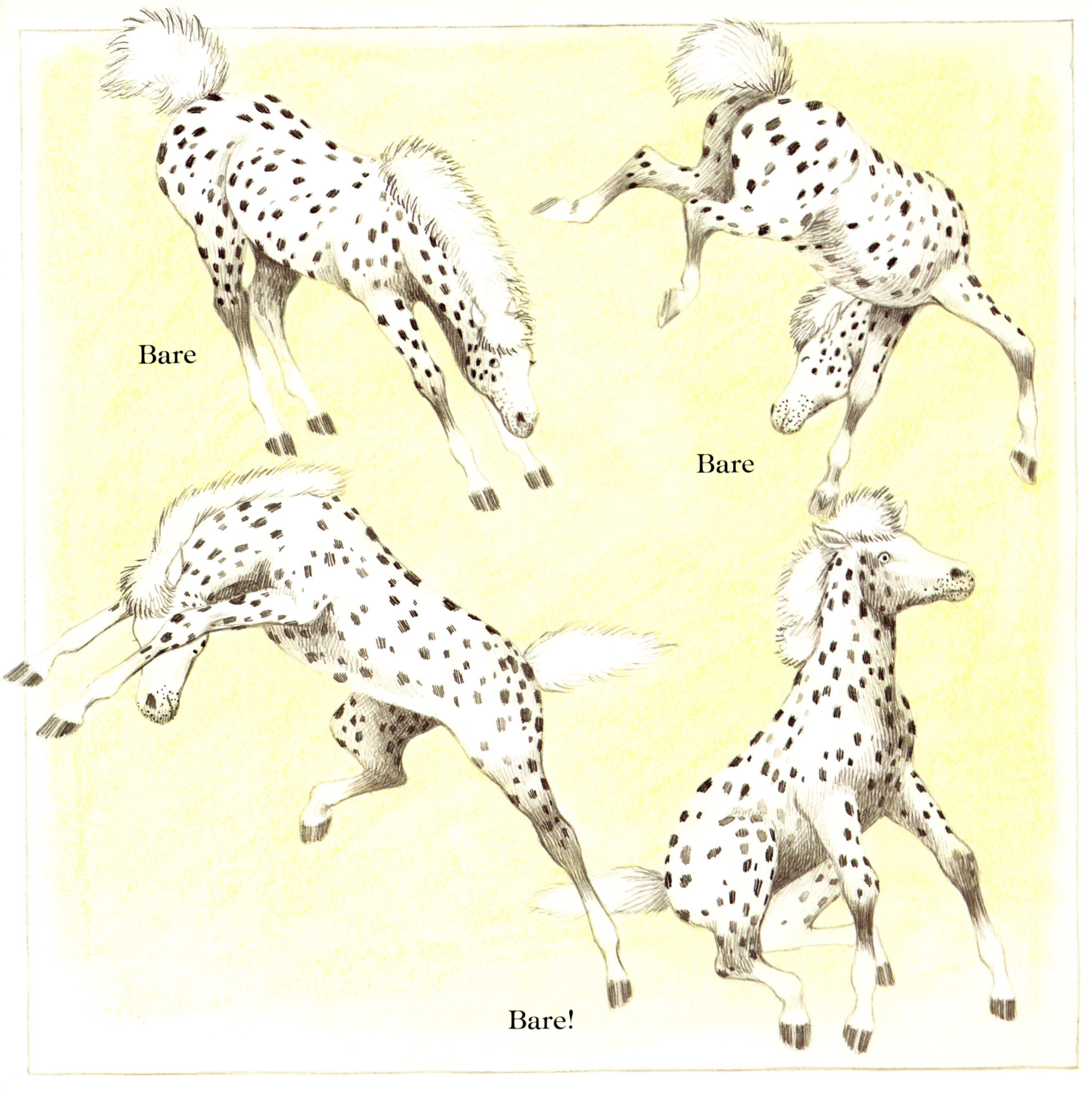

Ride a cock horse to Banbury Cross
To buy little Annie a galloping horse.

It trots behind

And it ambles before

And Annie shall ride

Till she can ride no more.

One white foot, buy him!

Two white feet, try him.

Three white feet, look well about him.

Four white feet, do without him!

Field horses, field horses
What time of day?
One o'clock, two o'clock
Three, and away!

The display type is Goudy Bold and Extra Bold photo-lettering. The text type is Tiffany Medium Alphatype. The art was drawn with a very fine pen and black India ink. Full color was added with a combination of pastel pencils and colored inks. The book was printed by offset at Lehigh Press.